THE CREEPER DIARIES

DIARIES

BOOK ONE

MOB SCHOOL SURVIVOR

THE CREEPER DIARIES

BOOK ONE

MOB SCHOOL SURVIVOR

GREYSON MANN

ILLUSTRATED BY AMANDA BRACK

Sky Pony Press
New York

Visit our website at www.skyponypress.com.

10 9 8 7 6 5 4 3 2

The Library of Congress has cataloged the hardcover edition as follows:

Names: Mann, Greyson, author. | Brack, Amanda, illustrator.
Title: Mob school survivor / Greyson Mann ; illustrated by Amanda Brack.
Description: New York : Skyhorse Publishing, Inc., 2017 | Series: The Creeper diaries ; book 1
Identifiers: LCCN 2016032680 (print) | LCCN 2017004459 (ebook) | ISBN 9781510718142 (hardback) | ISBN 9781510718234
Subjects: | BISAC: JUVENILE FICTION / Media Tie-In. | JUVENILE FICTION / Humorous Stories. | JUVENILE FICTION / Social Issues / Friendship. | JUVENILE FICTION / Family / Siblings.
Classification: LCC PZ7.1.M366 Mo 2017 (print) | LCC PZ7.1.M366 (ebook) | DDC [Fic]--dc23

Special thanks to Erin L. Falligant.

Cover illustration by Amanda Brack
Cover design by Brian Peterson

Hardcover ISBN: 978-1-5107-1814-2
Ebook ISBN: 978-1-5107-1823-4

Printed in China

DAY 1: THURSDAY

It all started with brussels sprouts.

Tonight is my first night at Mob Middle School, which has me kind of creeped out. It's a time when a guy could really use a pork chop—burned to a crisp, just how I like it. But instead, Mom served me brussels sprouts!

See, she's all into this new cookbook: 30 Days to a Greener You. Dad tells her, "Honey, you're as green as the day I met you." But that just makes her all weepy-eyed. Then they end up kissing or something. (GROSS!)

So let me say that I am not a fan of this green diet. Creepers don't eat brussels sprouts. It's not normal!

There's NOTHING normal about my family—except me. I'm pretty sure my egg was switched at birth. I have three sisters named Cate, Chloe, and Cammy. And not one of them is normal—not a single one. But I'll tell you more about them later.

My name is also NOT normal. It's not Colton or Cooper or Cody like other creepers I know. It's GERALD. I was named after my dad, Gerald Creeper Sr.

People say I look like *him*, but I don't really see it.

Anyway, back to the brussels sprouts. I would have fed *them* to my pet dog, except I don't have one. I have a pet squid named Sticky.

And if I tried to feed them to Sticky, Mom would notice the gross green hunks floating in the aquarium.

So I tried to feed them to my baby sister when Mom wasn't looking. But Cammy just threw them across the floor like bouncy balls.

When Dad scolded her, she scrunched up her face and did what she always does. She blew up. Yup, right there at the kitchen table. I almost wished I'd died in the blast and respawned somewhere else— like in a normal family's kitchen.

I call Cammy the Exploding Baby because she has zero control over her emotions. She blows up when she's scared or mad or sad—or sometimes just really happy. And she NEVER gets in trouble. In this family, that kid can do no wrong. Seriously.

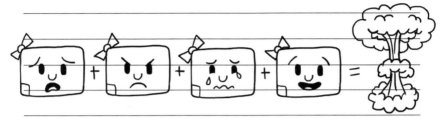

I thought that when she blew up, that would be the end of the brussels sprouts. But it wasn't. Mom just piled them back on MY plate.

When I complained, she used the old "There are starving mobs in the Nether who would DIE to have these brussels sprouts, mister."

I could tell she wasn't going to give on this one. So she left me no choice—I had to do it. I started rapping.

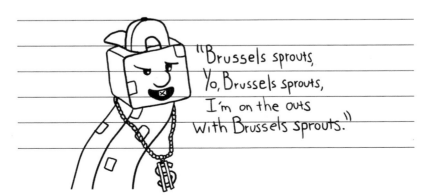

"Brussels sprouts,
Yo, Brussels sprouts,
I'm on the outs
with Brussels sprouts."

My favorite rapper is Kid Z. He taught me pretty much everything I know about rapping. And raps have gotten me through some tough situations.

I thought Mom would laugh at my rap, or at least get the point and fry me up a pork chop. Instead she did something I'll NEVER forget—no matter how much I try. SHE started rapping TOO.

We're going green, creep,
Going green,
Greenin' up
like a veggie machine.

She got all up in my face with these Mom dance moves. I tried to look away, but there she was again—creeping up on my other side!

Going green.
You know what I mean?
Eat your sprouts,
or I'll cause a scene.

Too late—she was already causing one. I shut my eyes, but I could still hear Mom rapping and dancing across the kitchen. And let me tell you, it wasn't pretty. I'm practically scarred for life.

That was when my older sister crept in. I didn't recognize Cate at first because she was wearing a red wig and pale skin. I call her the Fashion Queen because she likes to play around with makeup and different skins.

I think she's trying to impress this guy named Steve. She talks about him all the time. He must not be all that into her, though, because I've never met him. I'm not even totally sure he exists.

Anyway, Mom doesn't like it when Cate changes the way she looks. Mom said, "You should love yourself for the creeper that you are." Blah, blah, blah.

I took that opportunity to sneak away from the table. But for a creeper, I'm not very good at sneaking around.

"Where do you think you're going, buster?" Mom said right away.

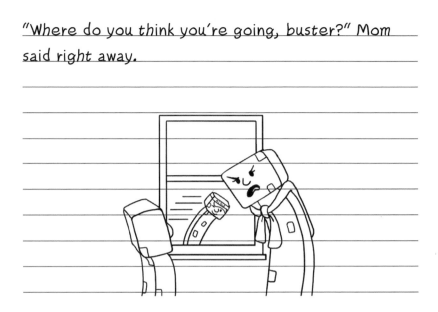

She made me go back to my brussels sprouts. But by then, DAD had somehow snuck away. I heard the front door click shut, and I saw a green blur pass by the window.

Have I mentioned that Dad is an excellent creeper? That's not a good thing when I'm trying to get away with something. He can pretty much SMELL when I'm doing something wrong, and he shows up out of nowhere—ready to bust me. But I can see how his skills could come in handy during a brussels sprouts dinner.

When Cate got tired of Mom giving her advice about boys, Cate started giving ME advice. She likes to do that—even when I don't ask for it. And it's usually about stuff I don't care about.

But today, her advice was about surviving Mob Middle School. So I listened up.

She said I just had to keep my head down and make it through the first two weeks. Then things would get better. She gave me all this advice about which mobs to avoid—and what would happen if I DIDN'T.

I don't know if Cate was trying to HELP me with school or just freak me out. But she pretty much freaked me out.

Then, when I thought things couldn't get worse, my Evil Twin walked in. Chloe flicked one of Cammy's burned brussels sprouts at me and said, "Hey, brother. Itch much?"

See, I have itchy skin. It's called psoriasis (SORE-EYE-A-SIS). I tell people that my "sis" Chloe is so

ugly, she makes my eyes sore. And she teases me about my itchy skin every chance she gets.

My twin sister and I couldn't be more different. I can't believe we ever shared the same egg! Chloe is always running around with her fuse half lit. But not me.

Dad says I'm a "pacifist." The first time he said it, Chloe laughed. "Gerald sucks a pacifier," she said, pointing at the rubbery thing Cammy sucks on.

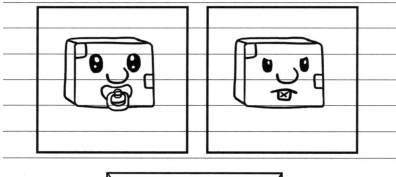

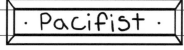

· Pacifist ·

But Dad says being a pacifist is a good thing. It means I like to keep the peace—that I use my brains instead of my blasts.

So when Chloe used my forehead as a backboard for a brussels sprout, I just ignored her.

Then she said, "Don't follow me to school tonight. I don't want anyone to know we're related." Like SHE was ashamed of ME.

"Nooooo problem," I told her. If she wants to pretend we're not related, that's fine by me.

So I guess I'm on my own at middle school. Which means I need a plan—kind of like Mom's green diet plan, except better. WAY better.

I need a SURVIVAL plan. I'm going to write it all down in this notebook. So here's my plan so far:

30 Days to Surviving Mob Middle School
- Keep a low profile.
- Avoid skeletons and spider jockeys (those jocks think they rule the school).
- Steer clear of zombies. They're gross and annoying.

· Never, ever look an Enderman in the eye. EVER.
· Come up with a cool nickname.

(Okay, most of that was Cate's advice. But the last part is mine.)

See, I know I can't change my family. And I probably won't change my skin, like the Fashion Queen does. But I've been thinking that maybe I CAN change my name, sort of. I can come up with a nickname, right?

I just have to think of the right one—a name that tells other kids right off the bat how cool I am. I have one hour to come up with something before school starts. And then I'll try it out. TONIGHT.

~~The Creepster~~

~~Creeper G~~

~~Kid Z~~

Kid G*

DAY 2: FRIDAY

Okay, so let's just say I learned A LOT at school last night. I learned _that things don't always go according to plan._

For starters, it's hard to keep a low profile when your new best friend is a super bouncy slime.

My OLD best friend was Cash. We did everything together at Creeper Elementary. He liked art and writing, like me. And we made up lots of rap songs. And I only ever saw him blow up once—when someone threw his sketchbook into a lava pit.

But then Cash moved away, and everything changed.
Sure, there are other creepers to hang out with.
But they're not like Cash and me.

So I was ready to go it alone at school. But Sam
bounced right over and introduced himself. He said,
"Hey, I'm Sam Sebastian Slime." He actually used
all three names, like I might confuse him with some
other slime named Sam.

You know what I noticed right away? That slime is
ALWAYS smiling. Even when a skeleton snapped the
strap of his backpack and sent him bouncing down

the hall. He just jumped right up with a smile on his face, as if nothing had happened!

But pretty much everyone else saw what happened so, like I said—there's no keeping a low profile with bouncy Sam around. I might as well cross that off my survival plan right now.

I know what you're thinking: Sam's cheerfulness might get annoying. I'm kind of worried about that, too. But since Cash left, new friends haven't exactly crawled out of the woodwork like silverfish. So that slime might be my best bet for a new sidekick.

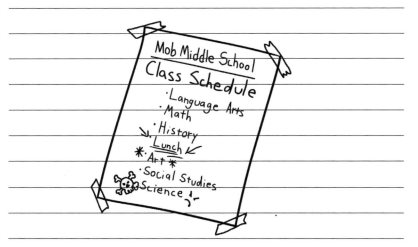

Sam and I compared schedules and figured out that we have three classes together: history, science, and art. Sam was WAY too excited about Science and not nearly excited enough about Art. But I decided to let that slide.

While we were looking at our schedules, this group of skeletons walked by and started messing with us.

The tallest, skinniest one, who I heard the other skeletons call "Bones," grabbed my schedule. He said, "Jeepers, creeper. Looks like a pretty full day. Want me to clear your schedule for you?" Then he crumpled up my schedule with his bony fingers and tossed it to another skeleton, and they started playing keep-away.

Bones probably wanted me to blow up, just to get me in trouble on my first day. But that wasn't going to happen. I almost told him I was a pacifist, but I'm pretty sure that word isn't in his vocabulary.

Anyway, he finally flicked the crumpled-up paper in my face and walked away, laughing with his annoying skeleton friends. I could hear their bones rattling all the way down the hall. Boy, was Cate right about avoiding skeletons!

She was pretty much right about ZOMBIES, too. This one zombie named Ziggy said something to me in the hall, but I couldn't understand him. He was eating a carrot and spewing chunks everywhere. YUCK. I got away from him as fast as I could, but he chased me all the way to math class. (Good thing zombies are slow!)

When we got to class, he staggered over to my desk and handed me my notebook. Turns out, I dropped it in the hall, and he was chasing me to give it back. Well, I'm grateful and all—I sure don't want everyone reading about my 30-day plan. But now Ziggy thinks we're FRIENDS or something.

During class, he passed me this note inviting me to dinner. He said his mom makes the best roasted flesh. I almost lost my brussels sprout breakfast right then and there. I really gotta ditch this guy.

Oh, and I learned that it's really, REALLY hard not to look an Enderman in the eye.

There's this one guy, Eddy Enderman. He's tall and cool and just leans against the lockers, like he's not scared of anything or anyone.

I tried to take Cate's advice and look at his legs instead of his face. But it's like I couldn't control my eyeballs. They just crept right up! So I pretty much have to avoid looking at him altogether. Too bad he's, like, THE coolest guy at school.

You know what else I learned? Brussels sprouts don't keep you full for very long.

I knew I'd never get through third period without a snack. So before Sam and I headed off to history, we hit the vending machine.

But it wouldn't take my emeralds! I could see the pork chops right through the glass, but I couldn't get to them. Sometimes I swear life has it in for me.

Then Sam stuck his emeralds in. And, of course, the machine took those—no problem. He got his milk.

I was about to protest when he told me that he wasn't TRYING to get milk. He actually wanted a cookie. But Mr. Cheerful didn't complain. He chugged the milk right down.

Then he told me that he's something called "lactose intolerant." Let's just say that means he should never drink milk. Never EVER. A stinky, green cloud filled the hallway, and I had to hold my breath all the way to history.

Believe it or not, keeping Sam away from milk wasn't my biggest lesson of the school night. That came during lunch, when I was finally ready to try out my new nickname.

I waited until the table was full of kids. Sam and I were sitting in the middle of a bunch of creepers, zombies, and witches. I paid him an emerald to ask, really loudly, "What's your name again?"

Then I said, "You can call me Kid G. You know, like the rapper—Kid Z."

What I didn't plan for was my Evil Twin walking by at that exact moment. "Did you say to call you Itchy?" she asked, snickering.

Yup, she actually teased me about my itchy skin in public. At SCHOOL. Around OTHER KIDS. I still can't believe it. I mean, I always knew Chloe was evil, but I never thought she'd sink that low.

I wanted to sink too—get swallowed up by a big hole in the ground. Where's Cammy the Exploding Baby when you need her?

I hoped no one had heard Chloe, but of course, EVERYONE did. And they thought I said my nickname actually WAS "Itchy" instead of "Kid G." I tried to tell them what I'd really said, but there was no going back—especially after the skeletons at the next table over got involved.

So now my new nickname is "Itchy," which I think we can all agree is NOT cool.

I learned a lot of things last night, that's for sure. But my biggest lesson is to avoid Chloe at all times. I mean, Ziggy Zombie is annoying. And the skeletons are bony bullies. But my Evil Twin did the most damage. I'm pretty sure a nickname like "Itchy" will stick around for a while.

So I might as well cross another line off my 30-Day
Survival Plan. It's starting to look pretty skimpy now.

~~Keep a low profile~~

~~Come up with a cool nickname~~

Oh, well. I can always try again with the nickname
thing when I get to high school—if I make it that
far.

DAY 3: SATURDAY

So Sam invited me for a sleepover at his house today.
And let me tell you, after another rough night at
school, I need something to look forward to.

The first thing I saw when I got to school last night
was a note on my locker that said, "Got cooties?"
I tore it off and crumpled it up. Then I opened my
locker. BIG mistake.

When I swung open the door, about a gazillion
SILVERFISH crawled out. They were everywhere! Kids
were screaming and running away from me, as if it
was MY fault or something.

I'm pretty sure Bones and his skeleton gang are behind the silverfish—they're the ones who started the cootie jokes. Anyway, I can still feel those bugs crawling on me. I had to empty my backpack, like, seventeen times to make sure there weren't any left.

Just the IDEA of those bugs crawling on me made me feel itchy. So I went through the whole school night trying not to scratch—for two reasons. First, scratching makes my psoriasis worse. Mom is always after me to stop scratching. Second, the last thing I needed was for anyone to actually SEE me being itchy.

I waited till the hall was empty, and then I rubbed my back like crazy against a locker. Of course, that's the exact moment when a group of witches came around the corner. They wrinkled their noses and ran away from me, like they were afraid they'd "catch" my itchiness or something.

So things are pretty much going from bad to worse on the nickname front.

Anyway, enough about that. Sam wanted to come to my house today instead of going to his, but I shot that down—for three reasons. The first reason is obvious. My Evil Twin lives in this house, and she'd have way too much fun ruining our sleepover.

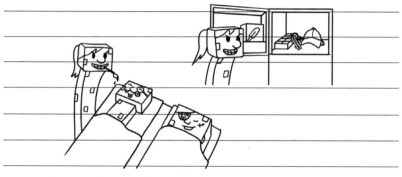

Second, Mom's cooking hasn't exactly been up to snuff lately. Instead of her usual "Burned This" or "Smoked That," she's still serving nothing but greens.

Chances are, Sam would just smile and gobble it all up. He'd tell Mom it was the most delicious food he'd ever eaten and ask for more. But I'd still be embarrassed.

The third reason I'd rather go to Sam's than have him over here has to do with bedtime. My parents like me to go to bed at the crack of dawn.

Creepers need their sleepers!

But I don't get it—it's not like we're zombies! We're not going to burn up with the sun. And neither will Sam. So I'm hoping his parents let us stay up a little later. Maybe even ALL DAY.

A creeper can hope, right?

DAY 4: SUNDAY

Well, the night started out okay. When Sam and his dad came to pick me up, my family wasn't TOO embarrassing. Except the Fashion Queen came downstairs wearing some stinky new gunpowder perfume.

I told Sam that Cate was trying to impress some guy named Steve. Sam said that her plan might not work, because Cate smelled like rotten eggs.

I don't really think Sam is one to talk, after the milk incident at school. But I let it slide. I've been doing that a lot with him lately.

Things were going pretty much okay until we got to Sam's house near the swamp. That's when three mini slimes bounced out of the house to greet us.

TRIPLETS? _As much as Sam talks, you'd think he might_ _have mentioned that he has three little brothers._

Let's just say that I'm not a fan of little kids. They're loud and germy. Those Mini Sams were oozing slime EVERYWHERE. I didn't want to touch anything!

But things got worse when we went inside the house. I smelled it before I saw it—a CAT.

Here's what you should know about me and cats: We do not get along. Not at all.

My friend Cash and I used to fling mushrooms at my neighbor's cat. Well, not AT him—just near him. He's an ocelot that Cash and I nicknamed Sir Coughs-a-Lot, because he's always hacking up hairballs.

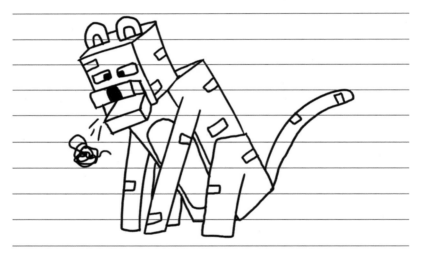

Sir Coughs-a-Lot doesn't like me, and I don't like him—that's a fact. We try to stay out of each other's way.

But as soon as I met Sam's cat, I knew it was going to be hard to stay out of her way. "Isn't she pretty?" said Sam, pushing the black-and-white cat toward me. "Her name is Moo. Want to know why?"

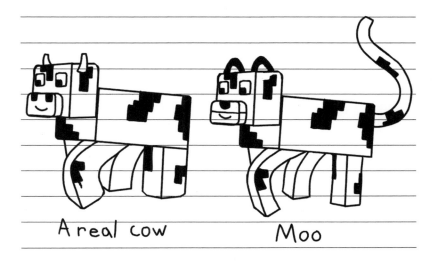

A real cow   Moo

I told him I could pretty much guess why.

Then Moo and I started doing this weird dance. She kept trying to rub up against me, but there was NO way that was gonna happen. I dodged her every move.

Sam thought we were really bonding, me and that cat. But it was all I could do not to start hissing at her. (And I am NOT the hissing kind of creeper.)

I finally asked Sam if he wanted to go outside. At least out there, I'd have a chance at losing Moo. Maybe she'd spot something more interesting than ME.

It turns out that Sam lives near some witch huts. Honestly, I was weirded out by those huts. They looked dark and empty. But when Sam said he was friends with one of the witches, I felt better.

Looking back now, I see that Sam was using the word "friend" pretty loosely.

We knocked on the door of a witch hut, and this girl answered. She wore this heavy purple robe, even *thought it was super hot out. And she looked kind of familiar.*

Sam was like, "Hi, Willow." But she just gave him this spooky stare.

When he said we knew her from school, she was nicer. But when she waved at me, I saw she was holding something slimy. A SPIDER EYE.

She told us she'd been brewing potions, and Sam was like, "Cool!"

That was not the word I would have used—unless "cool" also means "GROSS and COMPLETELY DISGUSTING."

I was pretty much done with this Willow girl, but Sam wanted to stick around. Lucky for me, Willow had a potion brewing in a back room that was going to bubble over or something. She said she had to get back to it. Phew!

As we walked back through the swamp, Sam said we should go home and play with Moo again. I could tell I was going to have to take control of this sleepover. FAST.

"Me and my friend Cash used to make fireworks," I said.

Sam didn't take the bait. But at least he started throwing out other ideas, like jumping on his trampoline.

That sounded better than bonding with Moo. But the trampoline turned out to be MUCH bigger than I thought it would be. I told Sam he could go first.

Now if you've never seen a big green slime bouncing on a big green trampoline, you really should. That slime bounced SO high!

When he came back down from orbit, he offered me a turn. But for some reason, I still wasn't ready. I told _him_ to keep bouncing—that I was working on a rap song in my head.

A cat named Moo and a witch named Willow,
How's a creeper s'posed to put his head on the pillow?
Slime's bouncing high like a planet in the sky,
Creeper's sitting down and he doesn't know why.

Sam wanted to help me. So he came up with this goofy rap right there on that trampoline.

Bounce, bounce, on my head.
Bounce, bounce, like a loaf of bread.

I try to be as fair as the next guy, but Sam's rap stunk—REALLY stunk. For starters, it was way too cheerful. Rap songs are supposed to be kind of dark. Plus, his rap didn't make any sense. When I told him that, he just smiled and added a couple more lines.

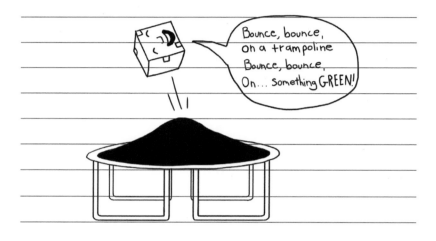

I figured there was only one way to put an end to Sam's rap. I asked him if I could take a turn on the trampoline.

He bounced right off, and I climbed on.

I've gotta say, bouncing on a slime trampoline is pretty fun. I bounced higher, and higher, and higher.

Pretty soon, I had a goofy grin on my face, just like Sam's. I was sure glad there was no one else around to see me.

We stayed on that trampoline until the sun started to rise. I waited for someone to call us inside, but they didn't. Sam's parents must have been too busy putting those mini slimes to bed. So my plan was working!

The sun was over the trees by the time we finally went in the house. All that bouncing made me forget about school and my itchiness. And I'm pretty sure I fell asleep with a grin on my face.

But it sure didn't last long. I woke up this afternoon with a cat on my head. ON. MY. HEAD.

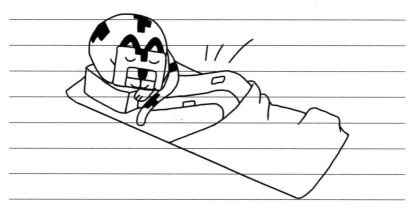

There's so much wrong with that picture that I don't even want to talk about it. I'm still spitting out hairballs.

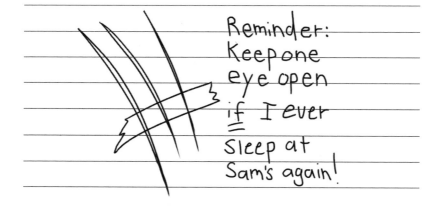

Reminder:
Keep one
eye open
if I ever
sleep at
Sam's again!

So next time? I'm going to suggest that Sam sleeps at my house, Evil Twin or no Evil Twin. A creeper has his limits.

DAY 6: TUESDAY

Sleeping with a cat on my head was pretty much a picnic compared to what happened at school Monday night.

I woke up this afternoon with an itchy rash on my forehead, thanks to Moo—not to mention all that scratching. Mom made me rub some coal tar lotion on the rash. Then she reminded me to take Sticky with me to school. My pet squid? I had no idea what she was talking about.

Mom said my sister told her it was "Take Your Squid to School Day."

I know that sounds crazy. At least, I know it NOW. But after my sleepover at Sam's, I was feeling pretty good about Sticky.

Sticky doesn't try to rub up against me. Sticky doesn't ever sleep on my head or give me a rash. Sticky just floats around in his aquarium, staring at me with his sleepy little eyes.

So I was *perfectly* happy to bring Sticky to school and show him off. After all, I have the best squid around. And maybe he'd take some of the attention off me and my itchy head. I grabbed the travel aquarium, and Sticky and I set off for school.

But when I got there, NO ONE ELSE was carrying an aquarium. And everyone was like, "What's with the squid, Itchy?"

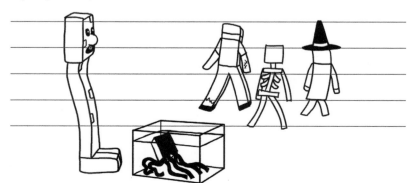

Even Eddy Enderman stared at me and Sticky. Normally, that would have been pretty cool. But carrying my pet squid on a day that wasn't "Take Your Squid to School Day" was NOT cool.

I ended up carrying Sticky from class to class.

Everyone was laughing at me behind my back—and sometimes right in front of my face. But what was I supposed to do? I wasn't going to stuff Sticky in my locker.

Then, when I was leaning over to check on him in the hall, Bones grabbed my lunch right out of my backpack. So to top things off, I was going to starve to death before the night's end. With my squid by my side.

At first, I was mad at Mom. I thought maybe she'd mixed up her days—that all those brussels sprouts were starting to go to her head.

But then when I got to history class, it all started to make sense. History is the only class that my Evil Twin and I have together. We sit as far apart as we can. She took a seat in the back right corner, so I sat in the front left corner.

But as soon as I sat down and put Sticky on my desk, my Evil Twin burst out laughing. Then I knew. This was no mix-up. This was just another evil plot.

I felt my insides start to bubble, like a pot of mushroom stew. If I didn't get control of myself, I'd start hissing—right there in class!

Sam could tell something was up, and he must have told Mrs. Enderwoman. She started class early and said she had something REALLY interesting to talk about. She looked right at me when she said that, which freaked me out.

Usually, Mrs. Enderwoman teaches us about the history of the Overworld. But today, she said we were starting a different kind of history project.

Mrs. Enderwoman said we were going to learn about the history of our families. "Genealogy," she called it. She wanted each one of us to choose a family member from the past to write a report on.

I wished she would quit using the word "family," because that got me thinking about my Evil Twin all over again.

Mom —— Dad

Cate Gerald ~~Chloe~~ Cammy

And the stress of it all made my head itch.

I started rubbing my itchy forehead back and forth against Sticky's ice-cold tank. I stared at Sticky. He stared right back. We were kind of in this thing together, Sticky and I.

Unfortunately, Mrs. Enderwoman thought I was shaking my head no. "Gerald, do you have a *problem* with this assignment?" she asked. GREAT.

I told her no and tried to sit still, even though my rash itched so much, I wanted to crawl right out of my skin.

The only good news was that Mrs. Enderwoman said our genealogy project wasn't due until the end of the month. That's ages from now, so I'm just going to put it out of my mind. I have way more important things to do before then.

Like STOP ITCHING. And figure out how to get back at my Evil Twin for humiliating me. But how does a pacifist get revenge? Too bad they don't teach you THOSE kinds of things at school.

After History class, I stopped by the vending machine to get some pork chops, because it had already been a rough day, and I figured I deserved them.

The machine actually took my emeralds. Woo-hoo!

But it spit out an apple instead of pork chops. SERIOUSLY?

I was staring at that measly apple when Ziggy Zombie caught up with me. Even if I'd seen him coming, I wouldn't have stood a chance. How's a creeper supposed to run when he's carrying an aquarium?

The first thing Ziggy noticed was the rash on my head. "Are those blisters?" he asked in a really loud and excited voice. He reached out his hand like he wanted to TOUCH my rash. Man, that zombie is disgusting.

I shoved Sticky in between us, and that did the trick. Ziggy pressed his green face up to the glass.

"Um, we gotta get to lunch," I told Ziggy. And for some reason, he took that as an invitation to come with me.

Sam sat with us, too—I was glad about that. But he was WAY too friendly with Ziggy. I kept trying to catch his eye and tell him to take it down a notch. We didn't want Ziggy thinking he could sit with us EVERY day. But Sam didn't take the hint.

When Ziggy starting eating some sort of flesh sandwich, it totally grossed me out. I got up and threw away my apple. Even Sticky spun around in his aquarium and looked the other way.

But Sam didn't seem to notice. He kept stuffing his green cheeks with cookies and blabbed on and on about who knows what.

When Ziggy asked what my squid's name was, Sam answered for me. He said, "Sticky" and blew cookie crumbs all over the table.

Well that did it. The skeletons behind us started singing a song.

They made kissy noises and laughed their bony butts off.

How old were those mobs anyway? I felt like I was right back in Creeper Elementary.

I decided to duck out of lunch early. The Art classroom would be open by now. And Sam had finally stopped talking to Ziggy.

But I must have said Sam's name three times before he heard me. He was staring at the other end of the table. When I looked in that direction, I figured out why. Willow Witch was sitting there with some eighth-grade girls.

What's up with Sam and that witch? Did she use a potion on him or what? I decided right there and then that it's time to ditch the witch and the zombie.

So "Take Your Squid to School Day" started out bad and got even worse. Guess that's Mondays for you. I couldn't WAIT for that school night to end.

DAY 7: WEDNESDAY

So tonight, I told my parents I wanted to call a Creeper Family Meeting.

I've never done that in all of my eleven years. But after the squid thing, it was time. My Evil Twin had stooped pretty low, dragging my mom into her evil plot. And I thought Mom would want to know about it.

Mom and Dad agreed to the family meeting right away. That surprised me—and kind of freaked me out. They didn't even ask me what I wanted to talk about.

Plus, they wanted to meet BEFORE dinner. Mom usually wants to talk on a full stomach. That's one of her rules, like not going to bed mad. And it's a good rule. I don't think anyone should have a serious conversation when they're hungry.

Like right when we were sitting down, I could smell potatoes cooking. And Mom hasn't made potatoes in a long time—she says they're too starchy. So as much as I wanted to rat out my sister, I kind of wanted to eat those potatoes, too.

This creeper was torn.

Anyway, it didn't really matter what I wanted. Dad cleared his throat and said it was time to get started. My Evil Twin looked nervous, which was good. Maybe she knew she was about to get busted.

The Fashion Queen had her red wig on again. She wears that wig so much, it's almost like part of the family—like another pet.

Sometimes I stare at it and think up names for it, like Rosy or Ruby or Ginger.

And the Exploding Baby? I put as much space as I could between me and her. She was playing with her blocks on the floor, stacking them in a wobbly tower.

Yup, there was going to be an explosion for sure.

So instead of asking me what I wanted to talk about, Mom and Dad started right in on what THEY wanted to talk about. And I was sure surprised to hear what that was. They wanted to talk about STEVE.

Cate was even more surprised than me. She almost flipped her wig.

Turns out, Mom and Dad found out that he's not a creeper, or a slime, or any kind of mob. He's HUMAN. Dad hissed when he said the name "Ssssteve," like it was a dirty word or something.

When Cate started crying, her makeup ran all over her green face. I felt bad for her, until all that runny makeup made my own face start to itch.

But my Evil Twin just looked relieved—like she was glad SHE wasn't in trouble. She thinks the whole Overworld revolves around her, I swear.

Mom sat next to Cate and told her everything was going to be okay. But that was pretty hard to believe when Dad was going off about how creepers and humans shouldn't mix.

#@!!

Boy, the old guy was really worked up.

Last year, I would have probably agreed with Dad. I didn't hang out with any mobs except creepers, and that was just fine by me.

But this year is totally different. My new best friend is a slime. Who has a crush on a witch. And the coolest kid at school is an Enderman.

So maybe humans aren't so bad either, is what I was thinking. But before I could say so, Cammy's tower of blocks toppled to the ground. Her face turned red. The screaming started. And we all dove for cover.

By the time Mom cleaned up the living room, the Creeper Family Meeting was pretty much over. I never got the chance to talk about the squid thing. But the look on Mom's face said that now was really not the time.

So I stayed quiet. I was still hoping for a roasted potato dinner before school started. Like I said, no creeper should have to face a tough situation without some food in his belly.

DAY 8: THURSDAY

This is the week when we're supposed to choose an extracurricular to do after school. And let me tell you, it's pretty slim pickings. Archery and sword fighting aren't for me. And spider riding? Um, no.

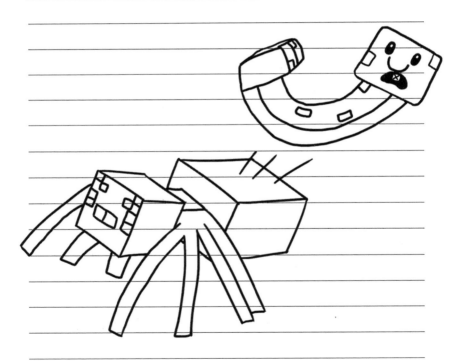

So that left sprinting, strategic exploding, and self-control. My Evil Twin signed up for the exploding class, as if she needs any help in that department. And I talked Sam into the self-control class. I figured that would be an easy one for a pacifist like me. Plus, I was hoping I'd pick up some tips for how to control my itching.

But when we showed up for class last night, we were the only two kids there. And our teacher was a zombie! Mr. Zane told us we were going to work on meditation, which meant sitting still and not saying a word for HOURS. At least it felt like that.

You know what happens when I'm supposed to sit still? I start to itch. And the more I tell myself I can't scratch, the MORE I itch. So sitting still was kind of out of the question. I kept leaning backward to scratch my back on a tree.

Also, I think it's pretty obvious that Sam can't sit still. He wiggles ALL the time. I kept nudging him to stop, but that only made him wiggle more. Then he started giggling. I can't take that guy anywhere.

To make matters worse, the spider jockeys were
practicing spider riding in the field right next
to ours. If seeing a skeleton ride a spider isn't
distracting, I don't know what is.

I kept watching them out of the corner of my eye.
I have to say, spider riding looks cool, even if the
jocks are a bunch of jerks.

Then I noticed Eddy Enderman leaning against a tree
watching the jocks, too.

So I started watching HIM. I wondered why he wasn't taking part in an extracurricular. But since they don't offer teleporting, I guess he wasn't all that thrilled with his choices.

Did I mention the strategic explosion class was going on in the field on our OTHER side?

After the third BOOM, I asked Mr. Zane how in the Overworld we were supposed to concentrate.

He said we should try chanting. But when he showed us how, it sounded more like moaning.

Ooooom. . . .

So now Sam and I were surrounded by spider-riding skeletons, exploding creepers, and a moaning zombie. I gotta tell you, I was really starting to regret this particular extracurricular.

That's when something hit the oak tree behind us. And an acorn plunked down and bounced off Sam's head.

We both jumped up and saw an ARROW sticking out of the tree!

One of the skeletons from the field nearby rode over on his spider. At first, I couldn't take my eyes off the spider. I'm not a big fan of those hairy beasts. But when I looked up at the skeleton, I saw that it was Bones—of course.

Mr. Zane recognized him, too. He told Bones to control his arrows, or he'd have to sit out of spider riding.

Bones pulled his arrow out of the tree, but not before glaring at me with his dark, hollow eyes. Even his spider seemed irritated. It could have been my imagination, but I'm pretty sure his eyes glowed red.

Did Bones think it was MY fault he got in trouble? Great. That's all I needed.

As he loped off on his spider, I noticed Eddy Enderman watching me. I almost looked him in the eye, but I caught myself just in time. Yikes! Why was he looking at me?

I couldn't concentrate for the rest of self-control class. I scratched myself silly. And I started poking Sam just for the fun of it. When he burst out laughing, our zombie teacher was NOT happy.

I really think Mr. Zane should have had more self-control and just ignored us. But he didn't appreciate it when I pointed that out. So by the end of the afternoon, Sprinting class was starting to look pretty good.

As we were walking back to the school, the other activities were finishing up, too. And somehow I found myself walking between my Evil Twin and Bones. I think that nasty skeleton was waiting for me.

It must have been my lucky night, though, because instead of bullying ME, Bones started teasing my SISTER. He must have figured out that Chloe and I were twins, because he said something like, "Well if it isn't Itchy and his sister, Itchy Witchy."

My Evil Twin lit up right away. It sure doesn't take much to fire up that girl, especially right after strategic exploding class.

She hissed at Bones that she WASN'T a witch. She probably wanted to say she wasn't my sister either, but that argument has some holes in it. So she took the opportunity to strategically blow up.

The blast sent Sam and I bouncing downhill. And I laughed all the way to the bottom. Want to know why?

Because I finally got my revenge—and I didn't have to do a single thing. My Evil Twin's own nickname for me backfired and came back to bite her in the butt!

Revenge sure tasted sweet.

But as it turned out, SAM was mad. He wanted to know why Chloe was upset about being called a witch. "What's wrong with witches?" he said. "I like them."

I corrected him and said that he liked ONE of them. And he liked her way too much, in my opinion.

Sam got all wiggly and embarrassed, as if his crush on Willow was some big secret. But I was glad it was finally out in the open. I asked him if that witch had used some sort of potion on him. Why else would he be so into her?

Well, that really got to him. He bounced away from me faster than I'd ever seen the slime move.

That was when I decided that we should definitely sign up for sprinting class.

I probably should have gone after him, but I didn't. My Evil Twin had just blown up, and then Sam had pretty much blown up, too. So I just sat there in the grass and enjoyed the scenery.

After all, someone around here had to show a little self-control.

DAY 10: SATURDAY

Sam did not invite me for a sleepover this weekend.
Was it something I said?

He was kind of quiet at school the last couple of
nights—not his usual bouncy self. And we didn't go to
self-control class because it was cancelled. The principal
said it was because there weren't enough kids signed
up, but I'm pretty sure Mr. Zane just didn't want to
deal with us. I blame it on the slime with the giggles.

When I told Sam we should sign up for sprinting, he
didn't really answer. Then I asked if he wanted to
practice over the weekend, and he mumbled
something about having to help his dad clean up the
swamp. Really?

The good news is, I'm getting plenty of practice sprinting at home—away from my mopey big sister.

Cate has been a wreck ever since the Creeper Family Meeting. She wanders around sniffling, hissing, and bumping into furniture. She still wears Rosy the Wig, but it's usually on crooked.

Cate isn't a big exploder—not like my other sisters. But lately, there's no telling what she'll do. For instance, when I told her she had her wig on sideways, she got all hissy.

Like it was MY fault she hadn't looked in a mirror lately. Sheesh!

So I left the house—quick.

I spent the night practicing sprints in the backyard. I figure if I can learn how to run faster, it might hide the fact that I'm not the sneakiest creeper in the cave. And it might be my ticket to surviving Mob Middle School.

But here's the thing: creepers aren't really known for their amazing running skills. I blame it on our short little legs.

So after one lap around the yard, I was pretty much tuckered out. Then, while I was leaning against the neighbor's fence trying to catch my breath, something hissed at me.

I thought it was a creeper—maybe even my scary sister with her crooked red wig. But then I looked down and saw Sir Coughs-a-Lot.

That cat was standing RIGHT next to me, and his back was arched. I don't think that's a good sign.

Well, let me tell you—I sprinted across the yard faster than an Enderman can teleport. I don't think my feet even touched the grass.

I REALLY hate that cat. But I think he might be my secret weapon in the sprinting department. If Sam and I use my backyard for training, we'll be speedsters in no time!

I can't wait to tell Sam on Monday. Hopefully that slime will be acting normal by then.

DAY 13: TUESDAY

Yeah, so Sam was NOT back to normal last night. He's kind of a sensitive slime. You'd think insults would just bounce right off him, but no.

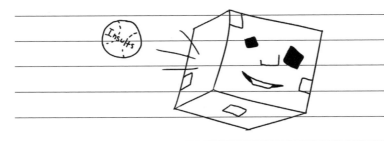

I'd apologize for the Willow Witch thing, except I'm fighting my own battle with Bones and his rattlers. And right now, I'm doing it alone. Unless you count Ziggy Zombie, who seems to be my new lunch buddy.

I blame that on Sam and his cheerfulness. We should have shut down the Ziggy thing the first time he sat with us, but Sam had to be all friendly and welcoming. So Ziggy keeps coming back around.

Luckily, the rash on my head is clearing up, so Ziggy has stopped being so fascinated by that. But at

lunch last night, he was chewing carrots with his
mouth open.

I turned almost completely around in my chair so I
didn't have to see it. But that put me face to face
with Bones.

Bones grinned at me and said, "Hey, Itchy. Where's
your pal Sticky?"

Man. You bring your *pet* squid to school for just ONE
day, and no one will let you forget it.

I ignored Bones, but then he and his gang started
flicking food at me. I could feel it hitting my back,

like little arrows. But I practiced self-control and didn't even flinch.

Then Sam showed up. FINALLY. When I asked where he'd been, he said he was carrying Willow's lunch tray for her.

Sure enough, the witch was sitting at the other end of the table with a tray of food. But why did she need help carrying it? She had two perfectly good arms, didn't she?

That's what I wanted to say to Sam. But I didn't. Because of the sensitivity thing. And because Bones had just chucked something at my head that felt an awful lot like an egg. A cracked egg.

As the egg goop seeped down the sides of my face, I looked at Sam. He hadn't even noticed. Boy, if a creeper can't count on his buddy during times like this, who can he count on?

That's when Ziggy got up and started wiping my face with a napkin. I sure hoped it wasn't the one he'd used to wipe his own disgusting mouth. But it probably was. Man, did my face itch after that.

Things got worse after school when I tried to talk Sam into joining sprinting. I don't know what his deal was, but he just flat out said NO. I didn't even know that word was in his vocabulary.

I told *him* how fast *he* would be—that he can bounce faster than most guys can even walk. But he wouldn't listen. Then I saw Willow coming toward us, and it all started to make sense.

Sam told me he was walking Willow home. She was going to show him how to use gunpowder to brew splash potions or something like that. And he actually sounded EXCITED about it!

That's when Bones rode up on his spider and started making kissy noises. Willow gave him the stink-eye, but Sam didn't seem to notice. He just bounced off into the sunrise with his witch by his side. That boy got bit by the love bug—bad. I sure hope it's not contagious.

Just the thought of liking a girl that much makes me itch. But these days, what doesn't? I gave my body an all-over scratch when no one was looking. Then I marched right over to sprinting class. I told the teacher, Mr. Carl, that I wanted to join.

I probably should have slowed down and thought about it. For one thing, the teacher is a creeper. And like I said, creepers aren't known for their sprinting.

Plus, as soon as class started, someone grabbed me from behind. I jumped so high I almost blew up, especially when I saw who it was.

Ziggy Zombie.

Yup, he's taking sprinting class, too. Lucky me.

So when people say they hate Mondays, I get it.
Hopefully tonight is a better night.

DAY 15: THURSDAY

I'm sitting in art class right now. I'm supposed to be molding a mooshroom out of clay, but I just realized something.

I'm halfway through my 30-day plan. And I'm not exactly rocking it.

Sure, I've avoided the spider jockeys, even if I think those jocks look cool riding their spiders. And I've somehow managed not to look Eddy Enderman in the eye.

But I'm still getting called Itchy by pretty much everyone. And instead of avoiding skeletons, I'm being terrorized by a whole gang of them. At least there aren't any here in art class. A creeper needs a little peace.

Bones isn't letting up on my Evil Twin either. He's got his whole gang calling her "Itchy Witchy" now.

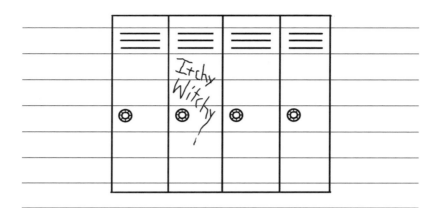

One of _them_ even used his bony finger to scratch the nickname into her locker. I heard that when she saw it, she almost blew up right there by the water fountain.

I don't know why she lets him get to her. The girl really needs to learn some self-control.

But secretly, whenever she and Bones are going at it, I want to pull up a chair to watch. It's about time my Evil Twin gets what's coming to her.

Sam is sitting next to me right now, working really hard on his mooshroom. But I gotta say, it doesn't look anything like a cow. It's red, but it's just a big blob.

When I mention to Sam that he might want to give his mooshroom an actual head, he turns to me with these gooey eyes. And he says he's not making a mooshroom—he's making a heart. For Willow.

BARF. Why do I even try?

Guess I'd better put this notebook away and work on my own mooshroom. When our teacher comes around, at least ONE of us at the table ought to have something to show for ourselves.

DAY 17: SATURDAY

So Sam got his heart broken last night. I don't mean the mooshroom heart he was making for Willow. I mean his real one.

If you've never seen a weepy slime, trust me—you don't want to. He was oozing green tears and snot EVERYWHERE.

"S-she won't even t-talk to m-me!"

He could barely calm down enough to tell me what happened. Then he got the hiccups, which made for a very bouncy conversation.

I guess someone wrote Willow a letter and signed Sam's name. It said all this nasty stuff about her and that he didn't want to see her anymore.

Sam found out about it from another eighth-grade witch. He tried to tell Willow that he didn't write the letter, but she won't talk to him.

I'm kind of afraid she's going to use some nasty potion on him, but I didn't tell him that.

Potion of Hiccupping   Potion of Love   Potion of Sneezing

The slime has enough to worry about right now—like how he's going to keep himself together instead of breaking into a thousand little sad, sloppy slimes.

I don't know what I'm going to do with that guy.
As if I don't have enough problems of my own! Like
steering clear of Bones. And outrunning Ziggy in
Sprinting class.

Oh, and I just remembered I have a big project due
in a week. It's that one that has me talking to my
family about our "history."

I don't know where I'd rather be right now: with a
weepy, snotty Sam or working on my history project
at home with all of my explosive sisters.

But Sam didn't really give me a choice. He said he
was going to spend the weekend in bed cuddling
with Moo. So I guess that's one decision made for
me.

History project, here I come.

DAY 18: SUNDAY

Boy, you sure find out a lot about your family when you ask the right questions.

Tonight, I told Mom and Dad about my history project. Dad got all excited and pulled out a gazillion boxes of old photos. He had pictures of creepers that were in black and white instead of green. If I looked at them from the right angle, my old relatives almost looked like Endermen. COOL!

With Dad's help, I put together a Creeper family tree. And there are some interesting characters

in my family, let me tell you. I don't know how I'm
going to choose just one to write a report about.

On my mom's side, there is . . .

  · A glamorous great-aunt named Scarlet who
     wore feather boas. (Mom said that must
     be where Cate gets her fashion sense.)

  · A great-grandma who tamed a CAT. How do I
     know? It was sitting in her lap in the picture.
     (But I will not be writing my report on this

person. I definitely do NOT want my classmates to know I'm related to a Cat-Lady Creeper. Just the thought of it makes me itchy.)

· A great-grandpa who got struck by lightning. His photo had this eerie glow.

On my dad's side, there is . . .

- A great-grandma who invented a way to turn creeper explosions into energy.

- A not-so-great uncle who blew up a village well. In the CREEPER CHRONICLE newspaper article, his photo looked more like a mug shot.

· A great-aunt who ran away to the
  Extreme Hills with her boyfriend, a miner.

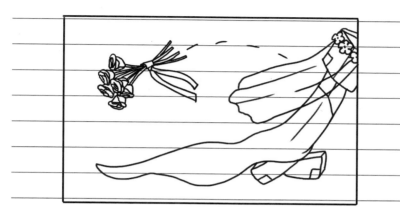

I didn't know Cate was in the room with my parents
and me. But when Dad mentioned the miner, she was
suddenly right in Dad's face.

When she asked why he was okay with his great-aunt
dating a human, Dad cleared his throat. Then he said
something like, "Those were different times, back then."

I could tell Dad needed my help, so I thought fast.
I dug deep into the box of photos and pulled one
out. I practically shoved the photo in Dad's face and
said, "Who's this?"

Cate crept off in a huff, but Dad looked relieved. He took a close look at the picture and said, "THAT is your great-great-grandpa Gerald. That's the creeper you and I were named after."

Right away, I wasn't very fond of this Mr. Gerald Creeper. If not for him, I might have been named Christopher or Cayden. But the next thing Dad said changed my mind.

He told me that Great-Great-Grandpa Gerald was a pacifist.

Say WHAT? You'd think my parents might have mentioned that to me once or twice. Like maybe when my Evil Twin was teasing me about being a pacifier.

I mean, I was NAMED after this guy, and I've never even heard of the creeper before. WOW. Makes me wonder what other secrets are hiding in these dusty old boxes.

I would have raised a stink about all that, except my Evil Twin walked in right then and asked what we were doing. When Dad told her, she got all wide-eyed. I think she totally forgot about the history report.

As much as she likes to pretend I don't exist, she pretty much needs me to keep her on track. You're welcome, is what I wanted to say to her.

Then I snatched Great-Great-Grandpa Gerald's photo right up. My Evil Twin can write about Cat-Lady Creeper or Convict Creeper, for all I care. But Gerald is all mine.

Dad started running through the family tree with my Evil Twin. She didn't seem all that into it, though. She said she was going to write her report on some guy named Herobrine.

Dad was like, "Hero who?"

And then Cate started to cry. AGAIN.

It turns out that Herobrine is some phantom miner who used to be human. So Cate thought Chloe was making fun of Steve.

I thought that was kind of a leap. But Mom took Cate aside and started saying all this stuff like "It's better to have loved and lost than never to have loved at all."

REALLY?

See, I know that's not true. I love burned pork chops. But Mom hasn't made them in so long, I almost wish she'd NEVER made them. Because if she hadn't, the brussels sprouts she makes now wouldn't seem nearly so disgusting.

But I kept my mouth shut. The last thing I wanted to do was get stuck in a conversation with my mom and sister about love.

Good thing I didn't, too, because I'm in my room now, and I can still hear them out there in the living room talking about it. BLECH.

Anyway, enough about all that. This creeper has a history report to write.

DAY 20: TUESDAY

Wow, I really did not see that coming.

Sam met me at school last night, and he started picking a fight. SAM. You know, the slime who usually can't wipe the smile off his face? Yeah, that one.

I didn't even recognize him when he bounced up to me all quivery and angry. He was almost spitting when he said, "You're just a sneaky creeper!"

Say WHAT?

Then he bounced away without even explaining why he was so mad.

I started sweating right there in the hallway. Did I mention that sweating is not good for my psoriasis? Stress isn't either, and Sam had just dumped a whole heap of it on me—for no good reason.

I had to hear it from Ziggy Zombie first. Ziggy said there's a rumor going around that I was the one who wrote the note—the note that broke up Sam and Willow's little romance.

Now, let's just get one thing straight: I did not write that note. I might have, if I'd gotten the idea before someone else did. Because I don't think that Willow Witch is all that good for Sam. But I didn't do it.

I asked Ziggy who started the rumor, and he didn't know. I guess it doesn't really matter. The point is, Sam BELIEVED it. And he stopped talking to me.

Mondays are hard enough to face. But last night was even tougher without that slime by my side.

In history class, I tried to tell Sam that I didn't write that note. But he wouldn't even look at me. During our quiz, I could see he was shaking—he was THAT mad at me. And I started itching like crazy.

When I leaned sideways to rub my shoulder against the back of my chair, Mrs. Eagle-Eyes Enderwoman caught me and thought I was cheating. So now I look even MORE like a sneaky creeper. And Sam didn't even stick up for me.

During lunch, I didn't see him at all. Ziggy scooted his chair close to mine and offered me half of his flesh sandwich. But the way I was feeling, I couldn't have forced down a burned pork chop. It didn't help when Ziggy happily pointed out that my rash was coming back. GREAT.

I went to art early hoping I'd run into Sam. But he wasn't there. We were dying wool with dyes made from flowers and bone meal. Can I just say that wool is a VERY itchy material? Somehow, I made it through class. But I must have been thinking about Sam the whole time, because I put some cactus in my dye and turned it slime green.

Sam wasn't in science class either. He must have gone home sick. We were supposed to memorize all the different ores in the Overworld. But how could a creeper think about that at a time like this?

Instead, I tried to write a rap song. That usually makes me feel better. But every song I started was kind of lame.

Lost my brother, ~~like no other, in a swamp of lies...~~

~~Diamonds? Uh-uh~~
~~Emeralds? Nope.~~
~~Give me Slime or~~
~~nothing, yo...~~

~~Ain't enough time to~~
~~find words that rhyme~~
~~With "Sam the Slime...~~

So finally, I just gave up.

DAY 24: SATURDAY

What a waste of a week. I should just scratch my
"30 Days to Surviving Mob Middle School" plan right
now and start a new one—a 30-day plan for making
up with Sam.

But at this rate, that might take a hundred days. Or
a thousand. Seriously, there might not even be
enough days in the Overworld.

I know—I'm being dramatic. But can you blame me?
Sam's been ignoring me all week!

Do you want to know how bad it's gotten? I'll tell you. There's a rash over my ENTIRE body right now. And there's something else, too, but I'm only going to say it ONCE. Here goes:

Ziggy Zombie invited me for a sleepover. I guess with Sam and me on the outs, he's making his move to fill the "new best friend" spot. And I'm in such a funk that I actually said yes.

Yup, you heard me: I said YES.

Wait, what? I said YES?

A zombie asked me for a sleepover, and I said YES? What was I thinking???

This fight with Sam has GOT to stop, or there's no hope for me. None at all.

I tried to get out of the sleepover, but Mom said that wouldn't be polite. I wanted to tell her that I've watched Ziggy eat lunch for three weeks straight now, and he's not all that big on politeness. But there's no arguing with Mom.

So I packed my survival kit:

  · My anti-itch coal-tar lotion. I'm pretty much taking baths in the stuff now, but I can't say that it's really working.

  · Snacks—and lots of them. You never know what a zombie mom is going to put on the dinner table.

· My book on squids. The way Ziggy looked
at Sticky, he'll be all over this book.
So if he wants to do anything boring or
weird, I'll just stick this book in his face.
Presto. New activity.

· My running shoes. Maybe Ziggy and I can
practice our sprinting. And I can outrun him
and just disappear.

The good news is zombies can't be out in daylight.
So this sleepover won't drag on forever. With any
luck, I can be out of there before dawn and not
even have to go to sleep.

So I guess it's not really a "sleepover." It's just an
"over." And hopefully it'll be OVER fast!

DAY 25: SUNDAY
Morning

Oh, man. I do not even know where to start with this one.

I guess I'll start with the good news, because there's not very much of that. The good news is that Ziggy's mom is a pretty good cook. Her roasted carrots and potatoes were right up there with Mom's (but I'd never tell Mom that).

I steered clear of the roasted meat though, because I couldn't really tell what it was. And it had this sort of rotten smell.

So that's the good news. I hope you weren't hoping for more.

The bad news is that Ziggy has a baby zombie sister. AND a pet spider. And I really don't know which one is more terrifying.

Threat Level ???   Threat Level ???

The spider's name is Leggy—imagine that. I guess zombies aren't really known for their brains or creativity.

Leggy stayed out of our way, which I was glad about. But I kept getting stuck in his webs. They were so sticky and ITCHY! Not to mention gross.

I still feel like I have pieces of web stuck all over me, which does not help with my itchiness.

So every time I got stuck in a web—and there were a LOT of times—Ziggy had to cut me out. And he was SO slow!

You'd think a guy with a *pet spider* would be pretty speedy with those scissors.

But there was nothing slow about Ziggy's sister, Zoe. That baby zombie zoomed around me in circles. She could even run through holes in the spider web and not get caught. I'm not making this stuff up—it really happened, even though I wish it were just a bad dream, believe me.

So when Ziggy asked if I wanted to go spy on some villagers, I didn't pull out my squid book and try to distract him. I put on my running shoes and said, "Let's go."

Ziggy lives near a village of farmers and miners. I don't get to see humans up close very often. My parents think mobs and humans should pretty much keep to themselves—which explains the Steve incident. So if I get a chance to spy on a few humans, I'm going to take it. Yes, sirree.

Ziggy led me to the edge of town. We hid behind a stone wall and watched the villagers finishing their chores.

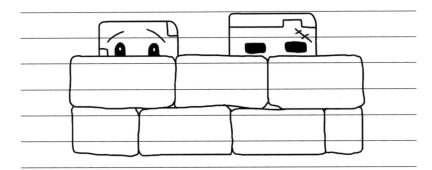

They wear all these different-colored outfits. It reminds me of the Fashion Queen, who is always trying to look like something else.

When I asked Ziggy about it, he said it's because humans aren't a very good color. They're kind of pinkish-brown—not a good solid green like we are. That made sense to me. Every once in a while Ziggy says something smart, but I don't say so. A compliment like that could go to his head.

Anyway, this one villager wasn't wearing robes. He wore a blue shirt and even bluer pants. Something about his clothes reminded me of Ziggy. When I looked at the zombie next to me, I realized he was wearing the exact SAME outfit! How weird is that?

I mentioned that to Ziggy—but I must have said it too loud. He shushed me, which I thought was pretty rude.

Everyone knows zombies are way louder than creepers.

Then Ziggy said the villager was kind of famous and that his name was STEVE.

Well, that just about knocked me right over. I made him say the name three times before I believed him.

So Steve was REAL. I was looking at the guy who'd turned my sister's heart into a green glob of mush.

I wanted to be mad at him, but I wasn't. He looked like a pretty nice guy. It's not his fault that my dad isn't big on humans.

Then I saw this human girl walk out of a shop and stand next to Steve, like they were together or something. And get this: she had RED HAIR.

All of a sudden, Rosy the Wig started making a whole lot of sense.

We watched those villagers until they went into their houses and turned out the lights. Ziggy wanted to make scary noises and stuff outside their windows. I guess he does that sometimes at night—it's a zombie thing.

But I kept thinking about Steve and Cate. And Sam and Willow. And all I really wanted to do was go home. So I told Ziggy about the squid book back at his house, and he pretty much sprinted all the way there.

When Ziggy finally fell asleep, the sun was starting to come up. So I snuck out of his room to make my getaway.

I wasn't expecting a watchdog outside the door—or a watch BABY.

Zoe was in a playpen in the living room. I guess baby zombies don't have a problem with sunlight. She was standing next to the window, happy as a kid could be.

But when she saw me, she wanted OUT. I guess she thought I was her ticket to freedom. I couldn't blame her. It would be a real bummer if you were the only one in your family who could play during the day.

So I did what any decent creeper would do. I hung out with her—just for a little while.

I sang her a rap nursery rhyme until she laid back down and started making sleepy grunts and groans.

Cootchy-coo, how cute are you,
~~Counting sheep and chickens too,~~
Sun comes up, and moon goes down,
Zombies snooze all over town.

Z-z-z-z . . . .

I guess having a baby sister has taught me SOMETHING (besides running for cover whenever that baby gets mad).

By the time I left, the sun was hiding behind some clouds. It looked like it was going to rain, which was kind of a problem.

On rainy days, all the mobs come out—even zombies. In fact, Ziggy probably woke up right after I left and wondered where I went. I'm going to have fun explaining THAT one tomorrow night at school.

But right now? All I want to do is go home and sleep. Baby-zombie-sitting is exhausting stuff.

DAY 25: SUNDAY
Night

Mom woke me up early tonight to say that Chloe was missing. Her bed wasn't even slept in.

I don't know why I have to be the one to go out searching for my Evil Twin. I'm probably the only one who WOULDN'T miss her if she actually went missing. But Mom said that if I found Chloe, she'd make me roasted potatoes for dinner.

I saw my opportunity right then and there. Mom needed something from me and was willing to COOK for it. So I turned down her offer and asked for something even better: pork chops.

Mom came back with (wait for it . . .) roasted potatoes. I guess she wasn't in the bargaining mood.

I accepted her offer. I mean, potatoes aren't as good as burned pork chops, but they're a whole lot better than brussels sprouts. So I set out to find my Evil Twin.

I looked all over our neighborhood first, but things were pretty quiet on the creeper cul-de-sac.

The thing is, I don't really know where my sister hangs out. I don't know what she likes to do. I don't even know who her friends are.

She wants to pretend that I don't exist. So I pretend she doesn't exist. And it's very hard to find someone who doesn't exist.

I *stopped for a moment and thought HARD. If I were my Evil Twin, what would I be doing right now?*

The answer came right to me: I'd be blowing up somewhere. And there's one place that's really good for that, a place where you can blow up without doing any damage: the strategic explosions field at school.

School always looks weird on the weekend, like an abandoned mineshaft. The building was dark, with no lights on. And the fields were totally empty. It kind of gave me the willies.

I looked at the oak tree that Bones hit with his arrow a couple of weeks ago. It seemed more like a couple of YEARS ago. I mean, Sam and I were actually still friends back then.

There wasn't an arrow sticking out of the tree anymore.

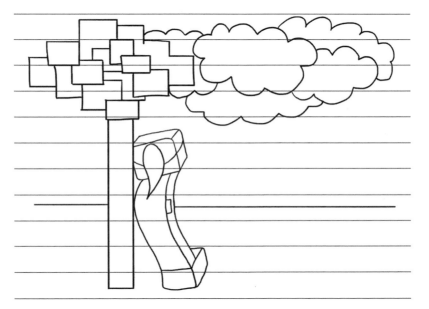

But there was something GREEN standing next to it. A creeper who looked very familiar. My Evil Twin. But what was she doing?

Normally if I saw her somewhere, I'd head in the opposite direction. But I had a roasted potato dinner riding on this. So I walked right up to her and asked in my nicest fake voice what she was doing.

I expected her to tell me to go away, or to call me Itchy and make some crack about my rash. Instead, she actually told me what she was doing. She said she was waiting for lightning—so that she could get HIT.

Well, what does a creeper say to that? All I could think was, did she hit her head? Was she hungry? Had she been bitten by a cave spider?

Lucky for me, she was feeling chatty. She reminded me about our great-grandpa who had been struck by lightning.

I guess after I left the room last Sunday, Dad told her how Great-Grandpa Casper had survived the strike. And he was super charged after that. His blasts were ten times more powerful than before.

So that's why she wanted to get struck by lightning—to get super charged.

She was just going to hang out by that oak tree until the storm came. As if it were the easiest thing in the world to get struck by lightning—and survive.

Now I had a couple of choices. I could have gone home and told Mom that Chloe was fine, that she'd be home in a bit (after she did her little get-hit-by-lightning thing). Or I could try to talk my sister out of it.

Because I'm a good guy, I did the second thing. I asked her why she wanted to be super charged. I actually complimented her blasts, which are pretty strong already.

I guess saying something nice to her helped. All of a sudden she was talking to me like we were BFFs. She told me she was tired of dealing with Bones, that she was going to blast him and his sorry skeleton gang sky high. As soon as she was super charged, that is.

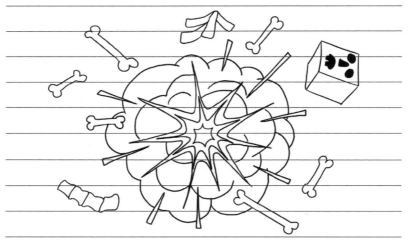

I couldn't believe it. My sister was going to risk her life just to get back at that bony bully? I thought that was crazy, and I told her so.

I said she just had to practice some self-control and not let Bones get to her. I even suggested she try some chanting. I don't know why I threw in that last part. Maybe I just wanted to sound like I knew what I was talking about.

Anyway, that was NOT the advice Chloe wanted to hear. She turned into Evil Twin again and said that I was a freak pacifist creeper who would never understand. I thought she was going to blow up right then and there. But she did something even worse. She started to cry.

I have never, ever, ever seen Chloe cry. Wait, maybe I did once when we were little and someone thought she was me.

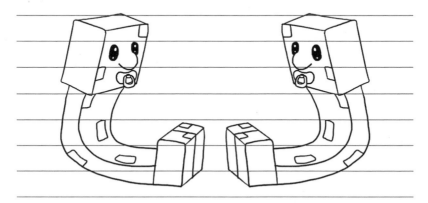

Being confused for a boy kind of rubbed her the wrong way. But since then? Dry eyes—all the time.

So this crying Chloe really threw me for a loop.
What was I supposed to do?

I heard thunder overhead, and then I saw that we
were standing under the tallest tree on the hill.
I guess Chloe knew what she was doing when she
picked this one. Lightning could have struck at any
second, so I told her we had to go home. NOW.

I couldn't believe she was risking her life AND mine
because of a stupid skeleton with a big mouth! She
stared at me for what felt like ages. Then she finally
ran away toward home. I think she was still crying.

When I started to run after her, I saw that we
weren't alone. There, leaning against a tree in the
spider riding field, was Eddy Enderman.

I almost looked away. That's what I'm supposed
to do, I know. Those are the rules. But right that
second, with my sister all upset because of Bones
the Bully, I didn't care about the rules. So I looked
at that Enderman—RIGHT IN THE EYES.

I knew _he_ could _teleport to me_ in a flash. He could hurt me, even worse than lightning.

But another part of me thought he might surprise me and want to be my friend. Maybe that was crazy—just like Chloe going in search of lightning was kind of crazy. But it was how I felt. And I was tired of being scared of Eddy.

So you know what happened when I looked at that Enderman?

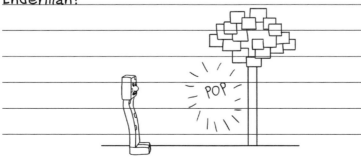

He disappeared. He must have gone the other way.

Some kids would have felt good about that, like they won the battle or something. But me? I was disappointed. It didn't help that the cloud over my head chose that very moment to drench me with rain.

I guess it's time to cross "Never look an Enderman in the eye" off my survival plan.

And I can cross out the idea of ever being friends with Eddy, too. He's obviously not all that interested in hanging out with a freak pacifist creeper like me.

DAY 26: MONDAY

The sun is coming up, but I can't sleep. I keep thinking about what happened last night.

Chloe and I made it home before the storm hit. And I got my roasted potato dinner. But it didn't taste nearly as good as I thought it would. I couldn't tell if Mom was off her game and had undercooked the potatoes, or if I was just off MY game.

I scratched my way through dinner, and Chloe just pushed her food around on her plate. Mom could tell something was wrong, but she didn't know what. And for some reason, I didn't tell her.

Normally, I'd jump at the first chance to rat out my sister. And if Mom knew that Chloe was trying to get struck by lightning, that girl would get grounded for sure.

But there was nothing normal about what happened yesterday. No one got struck by lightning, but we all changed somehow. My Evil Twin turned back into Chloe, at least for now. Eddy Enderman got a whole lot less cool. And me? I got mad.

I'm still mad. Not in a "hissy, I'm going to blow" sort of way. But in a deeper, tired kind of way. Or maybe I'm just plain tired.

Yup, it's Monday again. Did I mention how much I hate Mondays?

DAY 27: TUESDAY

I'm just going to jump to the good part of Monday
night. Which was also the bad part.

When Mrs. Enderwoman asked who wanted to
present their history report first, I jumped right
up. I wanted to get it over with. Sure, I have a
red, itchy rash over every part of my body, but I'm
tired of being afraid of being teased. And I'm done
keeping a low profile.

I marched to the front of the room and made an
announcement. I told everyone that my name is NOT
Itchy. It's Gerald, and I have psoriasis, and it's NOT
contagious. A couple of kids started laughing, but
Mrs. Enderwoman looked them in the eye, and that
pretty much ended that.

I told the class how I was named after my dad, who was named after HIS dad—all the way back to Great-Great-Grandpa Gerald. And I explained that Gerald was a pacifist, like me.

I even wrote that word on the board. P-A-C-I-F-I-S-T.

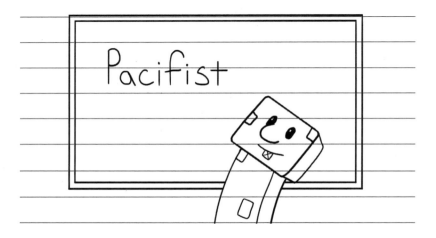

Mrs. Enderwoman seemed pretty impressed by that.

Then I talked about all the ways that Great-Great-Grandpa Gerald was a pacifist:

- He volunteered his time to rebuild houses that other creepers had blown up.

· He was a vegetarian. He raised *pigs* for riding, not for eating.

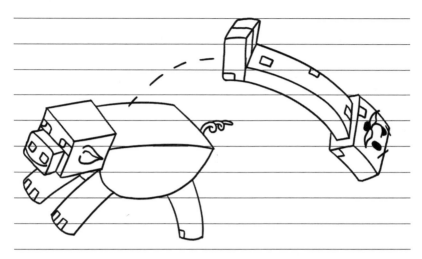

So *he probably ate a lot more brussels sprouts than pork chops.*

· He figured out a way to recycle gunpowder. Some of it was used to make fireworks!

· He helped plan the first Overworld Games. He invited mobs to come and compete at things like archery and sword fighting—like fighting, but in a peaceful way. And he invited HUMANS, too.

I saw some surprised faces when I said that. Even Sam's jaw dropped. When our eyes met, he looked away really fast.

I *thought my history report* was a success. I somehow made it through without scratching too much, and I was hoping I had put the name "Itchy" to rest. From now on, I'd be Gerald the Pacifist.

Boy, was I wrong.

But before I get to that, let me tell you how Chloe's report went. She stood up right after I did. Maybe I inspired her. But I could tell that her report was going to be too short. It was written on half a sheet of paper.

When she started talking, I sunk down in my chair. Her report wasn't even about a real person. It was about Herobrine—the phantom miner, remember?

Well kids started snickering, so many of them that Mrs. Enderwoman couldn't look them all in the eye. Chloe's voice got softer and softer.

When she was done, no one even clapped—except Mrs. Enderwoman.

I felt bad for my sister, even though it was kind of her fault. Maybe she didn't hear Mrs. Enderwoman's instructions at the beginning of the year. But she could have asked ME for help. That's the thing about Chloe—she never asks for help, even when she really needs it.

I followed her to her locker after class. I was going to say something nice to her, even though we never really talk at school. But when she opened her locker, something fell out.

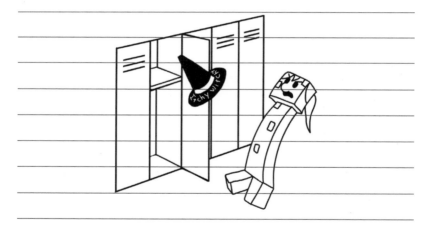

It was a black witch hat. And written along the brim was the name "ITCHY WITCHY."

I heard the rattling of skeleton laughter behind me. Before I could say anything to Chloe, she stormed past me and stuffed the hat in the trash. She didn't blow up, but she was gone in a flash. Then I heard an explosion coming from the girl's bathroom down the hall.

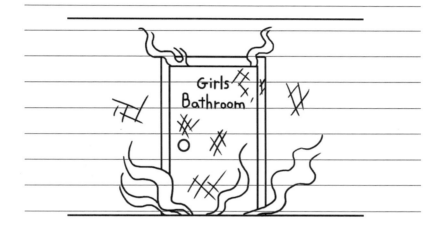

I whirled around, ready to face Bones and his crew. I don't know what I was going to say. Maybe I wasn't going to SAY anything.

That old bag of bones was already gone, but right then and there, something started burning inside me. At first, I thought it might be indigestion. Or maybe I was just hungry.

But after lunch, that lava pit was still simmering in my chest. After school, I could feel it bubbling. And even now, when I'm trying to sleep, I feel all shook up—like some sort of potion in Willow's brewing stand.

So this is new. And I have a really bad feeling about where it's all headed.

DAY 28: WEDNESDAY
Morning

I'm never going back to that school again. I repeat,
I'm NEVER going back.

Mom can make me burned pork chops lined up from
here to the Extreme Hills and back again. Dad can
talk about all that pacifist stuff till the cows come
home. Blah, blah, blah.

I'm not listening anymore.

Do you want to know how school ended this
morning? It ended with Mrs. Enderwoman picking
rotten flesh out of her hair. I guess she was
standing too close to the vending machine when I
blew it up.

Yup, that's right. Gerald the Pacifist Jr. BLEW UP. In the cafeteria. In front of everyone.

Well, now that I got that out in the open, I might as well tell you how the school night started.

It started with Bones calling me Itchy. Before first period even started. I don't know why that came as such a shock. I mean, Bones isn't in my history class, so he doesn't know that my name is Gerald or that I was named after Gerald the Pacifist.

And who am I kidding? Bones wouldn't care about that genealogy stuff anyway. He's going to call me Itchy till the day we graduate from this place. Maybe even after.

Like when we're all grown up and we run into each other somewhere. He'll have these bony skeleton babies with him.

And he'll say, "Kids, this is my old friend Itchy from Mob Middle School." Then those skeleton babies will laugh their bony little butts off. So I have THAT to look forward to.

But Bones has been calling me "Itchy" for weeks now. Why did it bother me so much last night?

Maybe because Sam was in the hall, too. And he didn't defend me. He wouldn't even look at me—even after I dropped all those amazing facts about my great-great-grandpa in class yesterday. So I guess nothing has really changed.

What happened after that? Well, fast forward to lunchtime. I was already mad because I realized during Math that I forgot my lunch at home. And I'm sure Mom packed me burned pork chops.

See, she said she'd make me something special after I told her I did well on my history report. And what else could she mean by "special"?

I didn't even get the chance to smell those pork chops. I forgot my green lunchbox on the counter, right next to Cammy's baby bottle. That Exploding Baby was probably home with Mom eating MY pork chops.

So I had no choice except hitting up the vending machine. Third time's the charm, right?

I slid in my emerald and hit the "P" button for pork chops. It took forever for anything to happen, like someone had cast a potion of slowness over the whole machine. Then a pork chop started to move. Not the apple or the milk or the rotten flesh (phew!), but a beautiful *pork chop*. FINALLY, something was going my way.

The pork chop dropped. I saw it with my own two eyes. But somewhere between the pork chop row and the hole at the bottom of the machine, that chop got STUCK. NOOOOOOO!!!!!!!

I started jiggling the machine. I know we're not supposed to do that, but I've seen Sam do it. He's pretty good at it, too. I guess I'm not. That chop wouldn't drop.

I kept at it, getting more and more frustrated. My entire body was itching, and I could feel the lava bubbling in my chest again. I knew the only thing that was gonna cool it down was that pork chop.

Then someone tapped me on the shoulder and asked if I was done because she wanted to get something out of the machine. "Do I LOOK like I'm done here?" I wanted to shout.

It was some snooty eighth-grade witch. I didn't know her name, but she reminded me of Willow. And I was NOT going to step aside and let that witch steal my pork chop.

So I just ignored her and kept jiggling the machine. Then I heard laughter. It was that tinkly-bone kind of laughter. I knew right away that it was Bones and his crew up to no good.

I thought they were coming after me, but then I heard Chloe hollering at them to STOP. They were ganging up on her, and she was fighting back. I wished she would just blow up already and get it over with. But for some reason, she didn't.

So I kept wrestling with the machine. I mean, I was really rocking the thing. And Chloe started crying—I could hear her. She needed my help. But I needed my pork chop. And Bones just wouldn't shut his bony mouth.

That lava in me was ready to blow. I got SO hot, like someone had just plunked me into a furnace. I was shaking, too.

When Mrs. Enderwoman stepped in front of me, I could see she was scolding me. Her mouth was moving.

But I couldn't hear a word she said because someone was hissing. It was SO loud. Then I realized the hissing was coming from ME.

I took a step away from the machine. I took a step toward Bones. And the next thing I knew, there was this huge explosion.

I heard glass breaking. I'm pretty sure that was the vending machine.

Then I was lying on the ground next to Bones.

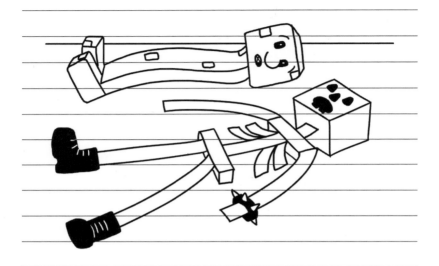

I must have knocked him over, because he had this really surprised look on his face. His mouth was gaping open even wider than usual.

Well, Mrs. Enderwoman and some other teachers cleared all the kids out of the lunchroom right away. I was glad for that. But I had to stick around and pick up the pieces.

There was gunpowder EVERYWHERE. I scooped it up and stuffed it in my backpack—no one even had to ask me to help clean up. I wanted to get rid of the evidence.

I wanted to erase what just happened, the way Mrs. Enderwoman erased the word "pacifist" from the board after my report.

She didn't scold me or send me to the office. She just swept up the glass from the vending machine and picked the rotten flesh out of her hair. Maybe she knew I already felt bad enough about my blowup.

Sitting through the rest of the school night was pure torture. No one would even look at me, except

Ziggy Zombie. I felt like an Enderman, but it wasn't nearly as cool as I thought it would be.

When that morning bell finally rang, I sprinted out of school. I sprinted as if Sir Coughs-a-Lot was chasing me. And I didn't stop until I got home.

I locked myself in my room, and that's where I'm going to stay. Forget about surviving Mob School.

Like I said, this creeper is never going back.

DAY 28: WEDNESDAY
Morning

Will this morning NEVER end?!

Dad just called an emergency Creeper Family Meeting. I'm guessing Chloe followed me home and told Mom and Dad everything.

So I can't crawl under the covers. I can't even stay in my room.

Everyone came out to the living room—even Cammy.

Then they all stared at me for a while, like they didn't even know who I was anymore.

That's exactly how I felt. Who was this Gerald Creeper Jr. who blew up over pork chops? Who beat up skeletons instead of using his brains and just ignoring them?

Dad was the first one to talk—no surprise there. He cleared his throat, which is never a good sign. Then he asked if I had anything I wanted to say for myself.

I shook my head. I'd pretty much said it all back there in the cafeteria. But I started to cry. I blame Chloe and Sam for that. There's been WAY too much crying around me lately.

That's when Dad said that what I did was okay. Just like that.

OKAY? How could he say that?

"But I'm a pacifist!" I reminded him.

Mom jumped in and said that being a pacifist doesn't mean you choose peace ALL the time. Just most of the time.

Then Dad said that no one is ever just one thing all the time. He brought up zombie pigmen as an example.

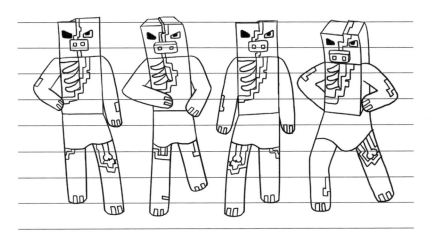

He said they're mostly really peaceful, but if any mob attacks a zombie pigman, they ALL show up for the fight.

Dad said that I went all "zombie pigman" on those skeletons because I was protecting Chloe. And he said that was a good thing.

I guess when Chloe told my parents the story, she didn't know there was a pork chop involved, too. And I wasn't going to tell her. I was just glad I wasn't getting grounded—at least it was looking that way.

Cate was sitting next to Dad, and I suddenly realized she wasn't wearing Rosy the Wig anymore. She actually looked pretty good—like her natural green self.

So after Dad's pep talk, I went a little "zombie pigman" for Cate, too. I said to Dad, "If no one is ever just one thing, does that mean ALL humans aren't ALL bad ALL the time?"

Wow. Cate's eyes just about bugged out of her head.

Dad cleared his throat and said that it was POSSIBLE I was right about that. Then he got up and said the family meeting was pretty much over. He snuck off before I even knew what happened. But then Cate gave me the biggest smile.

I don't want her going and getting her hopes up. I mean, Steve looked pretty tight with that redheaded girl in the village. But at least Cate seems happier now. And maybe Dad's coming around on the human thing, too.

So that was a pretty good family meeting. Cammy didn't even explode—she just played with her creeper baby dolls.

But if she HAD exploded, I might have understood for once. It actually feels pretty good to let those feelings out sometimes.

Just to be clear, I said SOMETIMES. I'm still a pacifist.

And I'm still dreading going back to Mob Middle School. But I'm trying not to think about that right now. A creeper's got to sleep.

DAY 28: WEDNESDAY
Night

Mom gave me a free pass tonight. Those were her words: a free pass.

She said I can stay home from school. But then she reminded me that the sun will go down again tomorrow, whatever that means. (I think it means that my free pass is a one-night deal.)

I've been sitting in my room thinking for about as long as a creeper can without going crazy. I tried to sleep, but I can't turn off my brain. It keeps replaying my blowup, over and over again.

Now I'm thinking about weird little details. Like, what should I do with all the gunpowder that I brought home in my backpack?

And what happened to that pork chop? Did the vending machine just swallow it up?

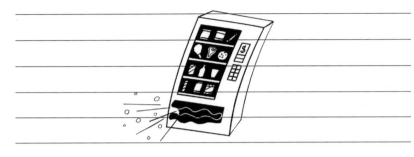

I really wish I'd found it, because after my big blowup, that chop was probably burned to a crisp, just the way I like it.

Anyway, these are the things you think about when you're staring at a blank wall.

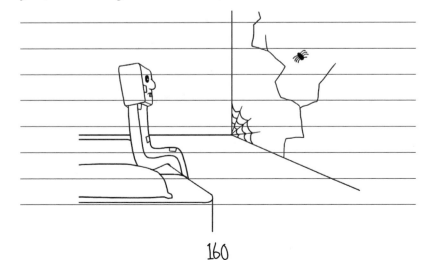

I really should _put up_ some pictures or something.

But not right now. I got a free pass tonight. And I gotta figure out the right way to use it.

DAY 29: THURSDAY

It's dawn, but I can't sleep. I did something last night that I've never done before. I went to the swamp alone.

See, my sisters were at school. Mom took Cammy to the park. And I felt like I needed to make a break for it, or I'd be stuck in my room for another twenty-four hours. So I grabbed my backpack and headed outside.

For some reason, my legs took me to the swamp. I knew Sam wasn't there—he was at school. When I saw the witch huts, I knew Willow was gone, too. But all of a sudden I was wading through the swamp water and right up to her front door.

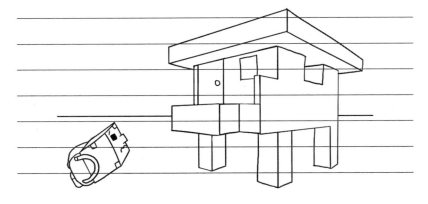

162

It wasn't until I was standing on _her porch_ that I knew what I wanted to do.

I _poured out all that gunpowder from my explosion._ I didn't want to keep it as a souvenir—it just brought up bad memories. But maybe I could do what Great-Great-Grandpa Gerald did and recycle it.

I _put the powder in a tidy little pile,_ and I left a note next to it.

Dear Willow,
I am sorry about you and Sam. He is a nice guy and you should give him another chance. I am also donating my gunpowder for your next batch of splash potions.

From,
Gerald

Then I hurried up and got out of there, because I was starting to feel like someone was watching me from the windows.

Now I'm back at my house, and I have to say, I feel better. I'm still not ready to face kids at school tonight. I wish I could wear a Jack o' Lantern over my head.

But at least right now, I MIGHT be able to get some sleep. Wish me luck.

DAY 30: FRIDAY

Wow. Somehow, my worst school night ever might have led to my BEST school night ever. Funny how things work out.

Last night started with a burned pork chop dinner. I thanked Mom for making it, but she said she DIDN'T make it. Chloe made it, as a special surprise for me.

Well I practically fell over when I heard that, but Chloe just smiled and offered me another chop.

I guess she wanted to thank me for standing up for her at school.

Then Sam was the first one to greet me at school. He bounced right over.

I looked over my shoulder, in case he was smiling at someone standing behind me. Nope. That big, goofy grin was meant for me.

Sam said he was sorry for thinking I wrote that letter to Willow. Turns out, it was BONES who wrote the letter!

I asked Sam how he knew. He said that after Willow got my note at her house, she used a potion of Invisibility to spy on Bones. She knew he kind of had a crush on her. And sure enough, she caught him telling one of his friends about the letter.

Anyway, Sam said he and Willow were back together now. Then he gave me a special gift from Willow: a bottle of splash potion I could use on Bones the next time he got in my face.

So now I'm thinking that having a witch in my circle of friends might not be such a bad thing.

I _might_ not even HAVE to use a potion on Bones, though. He didn't come anywhere near me at school last night.

But you know who did? Eddy Enderman.

He caught my eye, and when I didn't look away, he teleported right next to me.

I wasn't the least bit scared. In fact, I just said _hey_. Then I asked _him_ what happened to him last weekend in the schoolyard, right before the storm. I was still kind of sore about that.

Eddy just said that he's not a fan of rain—and he had needed to get home before the clouds broke.

Then it all made sense. Endermen can't get wet. I KNEW that! So I guess Eddy wasn't avoiding me that day. He just didn't want to get caught in the storm.

Anyway, that's not what he wanted to talk about last night. He said his mom told him about my history report. It turns out that his mom is Mrs. Enderwoman. Who knew?

Eddy said he was named after his grandpa, just like I was named after my great-great-grandpa. I figured that meant his grandpa's name was Eddy. But he said Edward was actually his middle name—that his real name is Louis.

LOUIS EDWARD ENDERMAN.

He said it just like that. Then he was gone.

I'm pretty sure that I'm the only boy at school who knows Eddy's real name.

Except maybe Ziggy Zombie.

Ziggy came up to me right after Eddy left. First, he said my rash looked better. He seemed kind of disappointed about that. Then he asked why I ditched him at the sleepover. He must have been working up his courage all week to ask me that.

I felt kind of bad about it, too. Maybe, in a way, Ziggy looks up to me like I look up to Eddy. And I really should be nicer to him, even if he has terrible table manners.

Anyway, what I'm trying to say is that blowing up at school might not have been the WORST thing I've ever done.

I still don't think violence is the answer. I think that whenever you can, you should make like a slime and try to let things bounce off you.

But every once in a while, you might have to fight back against a bully. Or a vending machine.

Just sayin' . . .

DAY 1: SATURDAY

I just realized that my first 30 days of Mob Middle School are officially OVER. And I managed to mess up every part of my 30-Day Survival Plan. Every. Single. Part.

Just in case you weren't keeping track, here's what happened:

- I did NOT keep a low profile. Blowing up in the cafeteria is pretty much a high-profile move.

· I did NOT avoid skeletons. In fact, I *hit* one dead-on during *that little explosion* we talked about earlier.

· I looked an Enderman RIGHT in the eye. But I guess that can turn out okay. At least, if the Enderman's name is Louis Edward.
· I did NOT come up with a cool nickname. Definitely not.

But somehow, I still managed to survive. Not everything turned out the way I wanted it to. But some things turned out even better.

Now, about that nickname. I'm feeling a lot less itchy now. Somehow, the explosion seemed to have cleared up my rash. But I know that people are still going to call me Itchy, so I'm going to have to find a way to make that name cool.

How can I do that, you ask? Well, I've been working on a new rap song.

It's going to a while to get it right. But like Mom said, the sun will go down again tomorrow. So there's still time.

<u>Here's what I've got so far:</u>

I'm Itchy, yeah, I'm Itchy...
Itchin' to be free.
You're itchin' to be you and
I'm itchin' to be me.

Bouncin' like a slime
Or rattling those bones.
Moaning, groaning, teleporting.
Anything goes.

We're all itchin', itchin',
Itchin' to be free.
You're itchin' to be free.
You're itchin' to be you and
I'm itchin' to be me.

Itchin', itchin',
Itchin' to be free...